Get **more** out of libraries

Please return or renew this item by the last date shown.
You can renew online at www.hants.gov.uk/library
Or by phoning 0845 603 5631

Hampshire
County Council

First published in 2009
by Wayland

This paperback edition published in 2010 by Wayland

Text copyright © Karen Wallace 2009
Illustration copyright © Cathy Brett 2009

Wayland
338 Euston Road
London NW1 3BH

Wayland Australia
Level 17/207 Kent Street
Sydney, NSW 2000

Series Editor: Louise John
Cover design: Paul Cherrill
Design: D.R.ink
Consultant: Shirley Bickler

A CIP catalogue record for this book is available from the British Library.

ISBN 9780750256070 (hbk)
ISBN 9780750258197 (pbk)

Printed in China

Wayland is a division of Hachette Children's Books,
an Hachette UK Company

www.hachette.co.uk

Mirror, Mirror!

Written by Karen Wallace
Illustrated by Cathy Brett

WAYLAND

Princess PJ was a tomboy princess. She hated wearing frilly dresses and fancy shoes. Princess PJ liked climbing trees and riding her horse.

Her mother, Queen Clemetine, on the other hand, loved to dress up.

She even wore her crown when she was picking peas in the royal vegetable garden.

"I'm having a big party tonight,"
announced the queen. "All the
important people in the land
are coming."

"That's nice," said King Crusty. Then he immediately forgot. King Crusty was very forgetful indeed.

"I shall wear my yellow satin suit,"
cried Prince DandyFop, who loved
dressing up. "I'll even wear my
high-heeled boots." He clapped his
hands in excitement.

Princess PJ rolled her eyes. How could her brother be such a wet lettuce? "I'm going riding," she said. "See you all later."

By the time Princess PJ came back,
Queen Clementine had locked herself
in her room, and thrown her ball gown
out of the window.

"What's going on?" asked Princess PJ.
King Crusty frowned. "Uh..." he began.
And then he forgot what he was going
to say.

"Mummy asked the magic mirror if she was the loveliest queen in the land," said Prince Dandyfop, giggling. "It said NO."

"What a silly question to ask!" thought PJ to herself. However, she didn't want her mother to be miserable, so she went to speak to the magic mirror herself.

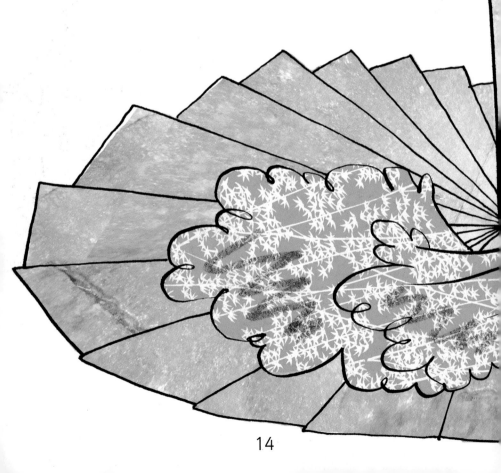

"If you don't tell Mum what she wants to hear," said Princess PJ. "I'll drop you on the floor."

"Okay, okay," grumbled the mirror. "I just get fed up of answering the same question."

"Right. Leave it to me," muttered Princess PJ.

PJ took the queen's ball gown
to the royal dressmaker. "This
is so old-fashioned," she said.
"Can you do anything with it?"

The dressmaker was delighted to help.
Snip, snip, snip went her scissors.

Princess PJ knocked on her
mother's door.

"Go away," sobbed the queen. "I'm just an ugly old hag."

PJ picked the lock with a hair clip and opened the door.

Three hours later, the guests had
started to arrive for the party and
there were people rushing around
everywhere.

Prince Dandyfop looked splendid in his yellow satin suit. King Crusty just looked confused!

Queen Clementine stood in front of the magic mirror. She wasn't wearing the old ball gown any more. She was wearing an amazing evening dress.

Princess PJ whispered in her mother's ear. "Remember what I told you."

Queen Clementine took a deep breath.
"Hey, Gold Frame," she cried.
"Cool or what?"

"Fabulous," said the mirror in surprise.
"Just fabulous!"

That night, the party was a
huge success.

The queen did look fabulous. Even King Crusty remembered to tell her so. And Prince Dandyfop was only a little bit of a wet lettuce.

As for Princess PJ, she wore something sparkly just to please her mother. Everyone agreed she was the loveliest princess at the party!

START READING is a series of highly enjoyable books for beginner readers. **The books have been carefully graded to match the Book Bands widely used in schools.** This enables readers to be sure they choose books that match their own reading ability.

Look out for the Band colour on the book in our Start Reading logo.

The Bands are:

🔖	Pink Band 1
🔖	Red Band 2
🔖	Yellow Band 3
🔖	Blue Band 4
🔖	Green Band 5
🔖	Orange Band 6
🔖	Turquoise Band 7
🔖	Purple Band 8
🔖	Gold Band 9

START READING books can be read independently or shared with an adult. They promote the enjoyment of reading through satisfying stories supported by fun illustrations.

Karen Wallace was brought up in a log cabin in Canada. She has written lots of different books for children and even won a few awards. Karen likes writing funny books because she can laugh at her own jokes! She has two sons and two cats.

Cathy Brett has been scribbling all her life – first on pieces of paper, on walls and sometimes on her sister! She later became a fashion designer and an author/illustrator. Her scribbles have appeared in lots of books, in shop windows and even on beach towels. Cathy likes listening to really loud rock music!